THE
FABULOUS
The Birthday Kitten 4

Adapted and Edited by
Jenny Cooke

HarperCollins*Publishers*

HarperCollins*Publishers*
77–85 Fulham Palace Road, London W6 8JB
www.fireandwater.com

First published in Great Britain in 1958
by Lutterworth Press

This edited and adapted edition published in 2000
by HarperCollins*Publishers*

1 3 5 7 9 10 8 6 4 2

Copyright © 2000 Enid Blyton Ltd

Enid Blyton's signature is a trade mark
of Enid Blyton Ltd

A catalogue record for this book
is available from the British Library

ISBN 0 00 274088 5

Printed and bound in Great Britain by
Omnia Books Ltd, Glasgow

CONDITIONS OF SALE

Contents

1

'What do you want for your birthday?'

'Children! You'd better begin to think what you want for your birthdays!' said Sam and Rosie's mother. 'Granny was asking me what you'd like yesterday, and Aunty Eleanor asked me today.' Sam and Rosie's birthdays were only three days apart, so they always shared a party between them and saved all their presents to open together.

'Oh! Yes, we'll think of our list straight away,' said Sam. 'Come on, Rosie. I've got a pencil. Let's put down Snap, shall we? Our old cards are so dirty!'

'Yes. And I'd love a new pencil case,' said Rosie. 'Someone trod on mine at school the other day and the zip broke.'

Sam wrote 'Rosie' at the top of one side of

his piece of paper, and 'Sam' at the other.

'Now,' he said, 'that's "pencil case" for you, Rosie, and I'll put "Snap" down for me. And I'd like a book about animals.' He wrote that down under his own name.

'I'd love a book about birds,' said Rosie. 'And I know just the one I want. I saw it in a bookshop the other day. I'll write down the title for you.'

'It'd be a good idea to put "book tokens" down too,' said Sam, nibbling the end of his pencil. 'Mummy, can we put down "book tokens"? Sometimes Grandpa gives us such a boring book, and I can't be bothered reading it and that's a shame. But if he gave us a book token we could go round the bookshop by ourselves and choose one we really like. That'd be fun!'

'Of course you can put that down,' said their mother. 'You always choose such sensible books. But put a few more things down besides those you've already written, Sam. You won't get everything you want, but at least there'll be plenty for people to choose from.'

'I know, let's put down a new doll for you,

Rosie, and a new train set for me,' said Sam. 'And what about a jigsaw or a computer game? And I'd love some paints.'

The lists grew quite long. Sam whispered to Rosie and she nodded.

'What are you two whispering about?' asked their mother, smiling. 'Something special?'

'Yes,' said Sam. 'I was wondering if it was any use putting down what we *always* put down and never get, Mummy.'

'What's that?' asked his mother.

'Well, we *always* put down a puppy or a kitten,' said Sam. 'Always. But we've never had one yet.'

'Last Christmas I put down "PUPPY" on my list three times,' said Rosie, 'and I got one. But it was a cuddly toy! It's lovely to snuggle up to him when I go to bed at night, but I really want a *live* one. Or a kitten. I don't mind which!'

'*Is* it any good putting down puppy or kitten again, Mummy?' said Sam.

'Well, I don't really want any animals till Baby Anne is bigger,' said his mother. 'And then, you know, they cost money to feed if you

3

are going to keep them properly. A dog needs a kennel too, because I couldn't have him in the house while the baby is so small.'

'I don't see *why*,' began Rosie. 'We could look after him. I'd love to.'

'Darling, you are at school all day, except at the weekends and during the holidays,' said her mother. 'Why don't we wait until Anne is bigger?'

'We've waited so long,' said Sam mournfully. 'I'm almost ten. And except for a hedgehog I kept out in the garden shed one winter, and a robin with a broken leg we kept till it mended, we've never had a proper pet.'

'I suppose then, Mummy, it isn't any good putting down a puppy or a kitten on our list,' said Rosie.

'Not while the baby is small,' said her mother. 'I don't want to trip over animals when I'm carrying her about. But what about putting down a canary? You could have that, if you'd like to look after it properly each day.'

'Yes! That's a brilliant idea! We'll put down canary,' said Sam, and wrote it down under both their names in big letters, 'CANARY'. 'It doesn't matter which of us has it, we can share it. I only hope we get a cage with it!'

It seemed a long time before their birthdays came. Their mother always made them a marvellous cake for the party. She was icing it in the kitchen when they came running in from school one afternoon.

'Oh! Get out of the kitchen quickly!' said their mother. 'You mustn't see your cake yet! Sam, look in the dining-room cupboard for me, please, and see if you can find a packet of tiny birthday cake candles. Count out eighteen. Ten for you and eight for Rosie, and bring them to me.'

'Birthdays are exciting!' said Rosie as she went with Sam to the dining-room. 'Sam, do you think we're going to have a puppy or a kitten, or perhaps even a canary?'

'I don't know,' said Sam, hunting in the cupboard. 'I haven't heard a whine or a bark or a mew or a trill at all, not anywhere in the house. Have you?'

'No. I haven't,' said Rosie. 'Isn't it a pity we like animals so much and haven't got any of our own, when there's Harry over the road who has a dog and rabbits and mice. And he really doesn't like them very much. He's always forgetting to feed them. It doesn't seem fair.'

'Lots of things aren't fair,' said Sam. 'But you can't do anything about it! Here are the candles at last, in this corner. I'll count out eighteen into your hand, Rosie. Amazing! Eighteen ! Isn't it a lot! I'm glad we were born in the same week and have a double birthday!'

They took the candles back to their mother and just as they were going out of the kitchen, they heard a funny squeak. They stopped at once and looked at each other.

'A puppy!' whispered Sam. 'I'm sure it was! Listen!'

They stood in the hall and listened again. 'Squeak! Squeeeak! Squeeeeak!'

'Well, it may not be a puppy, but it's something alive!' said Sam. 'It doesn't really sound like a puppy, or a kitten either really.'

Rosie went to look out of the hall window.

'The noise seems to come from outside somewhere,' she said. 'Listen, I heard it again!'

They listened eagerly. And then Rosie gave a

heavy sigh and said, 'Oh,' in such a miserable voice that Sam was astonished.

'What's the matter?' he asked.

'Can't you see what's making the squeak?' said Rosie, disappointed. 'Look, it's our back gate! It's swinging to and fro in the wind and squeaking each time.'

'Horrible old gate!' said Sam, very disappointed too. 'I'll go out and oil it this minute. Pretending to be a puppy and squeaking just like one!'

'Oh, don't get upset,' said Rosie. 'It's our birthday party tomorrow, and even if we don't get a kitten or a puppy, we'll have lots of other things. Let's go to bed early tonight to make our party come quicker.'

'Well, if we don't get some pet between us tomorrow, I'll, I'll, well, I don't know what I'll do!' said Sam. 'Something FIERCE!'

2

'Aren't there any more presents?'

The children's mother came into their bed-rooms the next morning and drew back the curtains.

'Happy birthday-party day!' she said. 'Even the sun has decided to make it a nice day for you!'

She gave them each a birthday hug and a kiss.

'All your presents are waiting for you down-stairs,' she said. 'So I know you'll dress at top speed this morning! *What* a good thing it's Saturday, and there's no school today! Well, to think you're ten, Sam, and you're nearly eight, Rosie! You *are* both growing up.'

The children washed and dressed as quickly as they could. As they got dressed they heard the postman come. What a loud rat-a-tat-TAT he gave!

'He must have lots of cards for us,' said Sam, 'and maybe some parcels as well. Oh, where's my other sock? I can't wait to get downstairs.'

The postman had certainly brought them a lot of cards. Eight for each of them and four between them as well. And there were four parcels besides, all looking very exciting in their brown paper.

On the breakfast table were other parcels, this time wrapped in pretty birthday paper, not brown paper.

'Hello, children,' said Sam and Rosie's father, and gave each of them a birthday hug. 'Happy birthday-party day both of you! How does it feel to be ten and nearly eight?'

'Well, no different, really,' said Sam. 'I always think there'll be a difference, but there isn't. Mummy, can we open our presents NOW?'

'Two each before breakfast, and the rest afterwards,' said his mother. The children looked at the parcels. It was quite clear that none of them held a puppy or a kitten. But perhaps one was waiting outside! Once when they had had a new bicycle given to them, it had been out in the yard. A puppy might quite well be out there too; in a box, or even a kennel.

They chose two big parcels and opened them in excitement.

'Wow! Look at this model sailing boat,' said Sam, his eyes shining. 'And I didn't even put it down on my list. Who gave this to me? Oh! Isn't it fantastic! Daddy, can I go and sail it on the pond this afternoon?'

'I don't see why not,' said his father. 'And, look, there's the card to say who gave it to you.'

Sam looked at it. It said, 'Lots of love from Daddy.' He ran to his father and gave him a great big hug.

'Daddy! *You* gave it to me. Oh, it's great! Cousin John's got one too, but his is only half the size of this one. Oh, what should I call it?'

'LOOK what I've got,' said Rosie, suddenly. She had been undoing one of her biggest parcels too. 'A new doll's cot! Mummy, I know

11

it's from you, I know it is. You said the other day that my baby doll ought to sleep in a new cot. Oh, Mummy, it's lovely. I can buy some blankets and sheets and a pillow for it if I get any birthday money.'

'Look and see what Granny's given you before you do that,' said her mother, and Rosie hurriedly undid the other big parcel.

'Oh, Granny's given me everything for the cot,' she said in delight. 'Look, Mummy, there's even a little duvet! Oh, won't my baby doll be pleased?'

Sam had undone his second parcel now, and he couldn't for the life of him think what it was. It was a long curved piece of wood, smooth to the touch, and sharp at the edges.

'Oh, I know what it is,' he said at last. 'It's that funny thing they throw in Australia and it comes back to your hand. What on earth do they call it?'

'A boomerang,' said his father. 'Yes, Uncle Roddy's sent it from Australia. He bought it specially for you. You'll be able to practise with it in the garden. Throw it at one of the apple trees and knock off the ripest apple at the top!'

'You really must have your breakfast now,' said their mother. 'Then you can open your other parcels. Sit down, both of you.'

The children sat down to their boiled eggs, gazing at the boat, the boomerang, the doll's cot and the cot-clothes. What a lot of fun they were going to have with them. And there were still plenty of parcels to undo. Really, a birthday was very exciting! But still at the back of their minds was a little worrying thought. Was there going to be a puppy or a kitten, or not? That would be much the nicest present of all, something alive, that they could love and that would love them. They listened for any bark or mew from outside, but they couldn't hear anything.

They opened the rest of their presents after breakfast. There was a magnificent new pencil case for Rosie, filled with pencils, pens, crayons and two rubbers; an enormous jigsaw between them both; a game of Snap for Sam; a book for each of them from Grandpa and, wonderful, they were the books they wanted.

'Mine's all about birds, the very one I was looking at in the bookshop the other day,' said

Rosie. 'Good old Grandpa! It's great! And you've got the animal book you wanted, Sam. Let me read it after you! And you can read mine. What fantastic pictures!'

There was a tin of toffees for each of them, a toy car for Sam and a lovely, little Spanish doll for Rosie.

'I know who she's from!' said Rosie, in delight. 'Aunty Kate, because she went to Spain and told me she'd brought back my birthday present from there. Mummy, I'll call this doll Juanita, and stand her on the mantelpiece, because she's good enough for an ornament. She's too pretty to cuddle.'

The children were really delighted with all their presents. They set them out on the floor and played with them.

'Clear up the paper,' said their mother, 'and I'll clear away the breakfast things.'

'Mummy, there aren't any more presents, are there?' asked Sam, still hopeful that there might be something alive, even if it was only a canary.

'Honestly, Sam, how many more do you want?' said his mother, stacking the plates together. 'You've both been very, very lucky.'

'There arenʼt any out in the yard this time, are there?' asked Rosie. 'You know, like our bicycle was once.'

'*No*, darling!' said her mother. 'You sound quite greedy! Now go and kiss the baby. She's not old enough to know why you've got all these presents, but you can go and kiss her all the same.'

The children went off to the little room where the baby slept by herself. She was awake and kicking all the bedclothes off.

'We didnʼt have a puppy or a kitten after all,' said Sam mournfully, as they looked down at the smiling baby.

'I know. And Iʼm really disappointed that we havenʼt even got a canary,' said Rosie. 'Iʼd much rather have had that than the lovely doll's cot. Still, we've got our baby sister and she's a bit like a pet, isnʼt she?'

'Yes, she's lovely,' said Sam. 'And she'd like a puppy too, I know she would. Oh well, let's go and put our cards up on the mantelpiece. We really have been very lucky, havenʼt we?'

'Yes,' said Rosie. 'And this afternoon there's the party to look forward to!'

3

'Oh quick, do something!'

The children enjoyed the morning of their birth-day party very much. After they had done their usual little jobs: making their beds, dusting their rooms and helping their mother in the kitchen, they were free to play with their new toys.

'I'd really like to sail my new model sailing boat,' said Sam, looking at it longingly. 'I was going to sail it this afternoon, but our party begins at half past three, doesn't it, Mummy?'

'Yes, dear. And you'll have to blow up the balloons for me,' said his mother, 'and bring some bedroom chairs down for the dining-room because we shan't have enough. And I want Rosie to pick some flowers out of the garden and arrange them in the vases for me, to make the rooms look nice.'

'Mummy, we'll do all that,' said Sam. 'No problem. But it really won't take us long. Couldn't we take my boat to sail on the pond this morning?'

'I want to make up my new doll's cot first,' said Rosie. 'I can't wait to make the bed and put that little pink duvet on top. My baby doll is very, very pleased with it, Mummy!'

Her mother laughed. 'I'm sure she is. Well, look now, why don't you do all my little jobs and make up your doll's cot quickly? And then you'll be ready to go to the pond with Sam. He really is longing to sail his model boat. You'll need some string, Sam, won't you? The pond is big, and if the wind blows hard, it might take your boat right out into the middle of the water.'

'Will we be all right going on our own?' asked Rosie.

'Well,' said Mummy, 'Aunty Eleanor told me that she and Uncle Jim and John and Sarah are going up there this morning for a walk. I'll give her a ring and ask her to keep an eye on you two as well.'

Rosie grinned.

'The Fabulous Four will be together again!' she said.

'Fantastic!' said Sam.

'Sam, *have* you got some string?' asked his mother.

'Yes, plenty,' said Sam, patting his pocket. 'OK then. We'll hurry up and do everything, Mummy, and then go to the pond. Can we take the baby in her pram?'

'No, not by the pond,' said Mummy. 'I do trust you, you know that, but it would be dreadful if the pram ran down into the pond. I'll keep the baby here.'

It wasn't long before the children had done everything and Rosie had made up her new doll's cot beautifully, and put the baby doll into it. She looked so peaceful, lying there with her eyes shut. Baby Anne was in her pram, lying peacefully with *her* eyes shut too. Rosie wished they could take her to the pond as well. She did so like being with them. She picked up the baby's soft yellow duck, and put it near her hand.

'She loves it, but she's always throwing it over the side of her pram!' said Rosie. 'I've picked it up about a hundred times, I should think! Are you ready, Sam? Is it heavy to carry your new model sailing boat? It's so big!'

'I don't care how heavy it is,' said Sam, proudly. 'I *like* carrying it! Won't all the children stare at us when we meet them. Come on, Rosie.'

The other children certainly did stare when they saw the big model sailing boat Sam was carrying. Harry came up and wanted to carry it for him. But Sam wouldn't let him. Nobody else was going to carry his birthday boat that day!

It was quite a long way to the pond. They had to go up the hill and down again, round the corner and then, lying at the edge of a field, there was the pond. It was a nice big one, and it usually had ducks on it but this morning there were none. It was fairly deep in the middle, and would have been nicer if only people hadn't thrown rubbish into it. There was a tin kettle, two old cans and a wooden box that bobbed up and down. They spoilt the pretty pond.

'Now we'll see how my new boat sails,' said Sam in delight. 'I've decided to call her the

Flying Swan, Rosie. Do you think that's a good name?'

'Oh, *yes*,' said Rosie. 'Model boats do look rather like swans when they are sailing along. It's a lovely name.'

'Do you think Aunty Eleanor and Uncle Jim are here yet?' asked Sam.

Rosie looked around for their aunt and uncle and two cousins, John and Sarah.

'No, they're not,' she said.

Sam looked at his watch.

'I expect we're a bit too early for them,' he said. 'Never mind. There are a few other grown-ups about and I don't expect they'll be long. I don't think Mummy will mind if we start sailing the boat now. I just can't wait!'

Soon the boat was on the pond. It floated beautifully and didn't flop on its side at all, as some model boats do.

'Look at her!' said Sam in delight. 'Just look at how she's bobbing over the little ripples! Look how the wind is filling her sails like a real ship! She's speeding over the water exactly like those tall ships we once saw at the seaside.'

21

The boat really was a fine sight to watch. She sailed over the pond right to the very end of her string, and then, when Sam pulled at her gently, she turned and came back again as steady as could be.

'Let me hold her now,' said Rosie, and Sam gave her the string. Rosie liked to feel the boat pulling at her hand as she sailed here and there. 'She feels alive when the string pulls on my finger,' she said. 'Oh, look, Sam, is one of her sails coming loose? Yes, look, it's gone all crooked.'

'Let me have the string,' said Sam at once. 'I expect a knot has come loose.' He took the string from Rosie and pulled the boat in carefully.

'Yes, it's just a knot that wants tying up,' he said. 'Let's go and sit down by that bush and I can do it properly.' So they took the boat to the big bush and sat down. The knot was very awkward to tie and the two children bent their heads over the boat, lost in what they were doing.

They didn't see a big boy come up and look all around. He didn't see them either, for the bush hid them, and they weren't making a sound. He carried something tied up in an old flour bag, and he had hidden it under his jacket. He didn't come right down to the edge of the pond, but stood a little way away, still looking cautiously all around. Then he raised his arm and threw the flour bag straight over the water of the pond.

SPLASH!

The noise made the children lift their heads at once and stare at the pond.

'What was that?' asked Sam. 'What fell into the water just then?'

'I don't know,' said Rosie, puzzled. 'I didn't see anything. And there's nobody about. Perhaps it was a fish or a frog jumping.'

'Look! What's that over there, in the middle of the pond?' asked Sam. 'It's something moving. Whatever can it be?'

Then a noise came to their ears, a high-pitched squeak, and the thing in the pond began to roll over and over.

'Look! See that bag, or whatever it is?' said Sam, leaping up. 'That's what fell, or was thrown in. And there's something in it, Rosie! Something alive!'

23

'Oh, quick! Do something!' cried Rosie. 'It'll drown! It's struggling so much, but it can't get out of the bag.'

Sam tore off his shoes and socks and waded into the water. The bottom of the pond was muddy and his feet sank into it as he waded.

'Oh, do be careful,' cried Rosie, looking round anxiously for her aunt.

The water soon came over his knees, but at last he managed to reach out to the struggling thing near him and picked it up. At once he felt a wriggling, frantic little body inside. What could it be? What *could* it be?

4

'We really must get help!'

'Rosie! There's something inside this bag!' cried Sam. 'It feels like some tiny animal. Oh, how *could* anyone do such a cruel thing! Fancy tying it up and then throwing it away to drown!'

He waded to shore, holding the wriggling little thing in the bag as gently as he could. It struggled and squeaked in terror.

'What is it? Oh Sam, poor little thing! Undo the knots tying up the bag!' cried Rosie. 'Who threw it into the pond? I never heard anyone come. I only heard the splash.'

'I can't undo these knots,' said Sam, sitting down to try again. 'The string is so wet. Rosie, you try.'

Rosie took the bag, and while Sam dried his feet on the grass and put his socks and shoes back on again, she soon had the knots undone. The mouth of the old flour bag fell open. And a tiny white tail appeared.

'Look, there's its tail,' said Rosie. 'What a tiny creature, no bigger than a rat. It isn't a white rat, is it, Sam? Be careful the poor thing doesn't bite you.'

Very gently indeed Sam pulled the tiny creature out of the dripping wet bag. At first the children could not make out what it was, it was so wet and bedraggled and small. Then a tiny mew came from the little thing and they both knew at once what it was.

'A *kitten!* A tiny, tiny kitten,' said Rosie. 'A white one. Oh, poor little thing, it's so frightened. It can't be more than two or three weeks old. Has it got its eyes open? It's so wet and miserable, I can't tell.'

'We'd better take it home and dry it at once,' said Sam. 'It ought to be put somewhere warm, it's shivering. What a pity the sun's just gone in! Oh, poor, little frightened thing, we'll do what we can for you.'

'Give it to me,' said Rosie. 'I'll dry it gently with my hanky and then I'll put it inside my jumper and hold it there. It'll be warm then. What a tiny, tiny mew it has.'

Sam gave the kitten to her and watched his sister dry the little thing with her handkerchief. It didn't seem to like it much, and mewed again. But it liked it when Rosie put it carefully under her soft woollen jumper and held it there safely. It stopped mewing at once.

Just then Sam noticed Aunty Eleanor and Uncle Jim, with John and Sarah, over on the other side of the pond, waving to them. He waved back.

'You get your boat,' said Rosie. 'We left it there, by the bush. You don't want to sail it any more, do you?'

'No,' said Sam. 'I want to get this kitten home and safe. What do you think Mummy will say, Rosie?'

Rosie was silent. What *would* their mother say? She didn't want pets in the house while she had the baby to carry about, up and down stairs. And certainly it would be dreadful if she fell over a kitten on the stairs with Anne in her arms. But how could they do anything but take it home?

'We can't tell Mummy *today*,' said Sam. 'She has a lot to do because it's our birthday party this afternoon. Do you think Aunty Eleanor would help us?'

'Yes,' said Rosie, 'but she'd still have to tell Mummy. Maybe we could whisper it to John and Sarah and they might help.'

'Well yes, but there's still the problem of where to put it,' said Sam.

'Not in the house, because Mummy would hear it squeaking,' said Rosie. 'It would have to be somewhere outside.'

'I know, let's put it in the old shed,' said Sam. 'Nobody ever goes there except us, now Daddy has built a new shed. There's only our bicycles there, and our old spades and things. We could make a bed for the kitten in there.'

'What about feeding it?' said Rosie. 'How do we feed it? And I wonder how old it is? Shouldn't its mother still be feeding it? Oh, help! What a lot of difficulties there are.'

'Isn't there anyone we could ask?' said Sam. 'Someone who knows about animals? We've never had any, so we don't really know. What about Harry? His father is a vet. You know, like the animal doctor on television!'

'Yes,' said Rosie, 'the vet, Mr Williams. He went to Farmer Hill when his horses were ill, and he mended the leg of Mrs Brown's dog when he got run over. And he took a thorn out of Hilary's cat's front paw. I was there when he did that and he's nice. Yes, let's ask Harry if he knows anything about tiny kittens.'

'Well, if my father was a vet I'd know lots about animals,' said Sam. 'I'd love to learn. Let's go to Harry's house now and see if he's in.'

On the way they saw their aunt and uncle and two cousins again. John ran over.

'See you this afternoon at the party,' he said, staring at Rosie who was clutching the kitten under her jumper.

'Yes,' said Sam. 'We've got to hurry now, but we'll tell you all about it this afternoon!'

So they went to Harry Williams' house and walked round the back to find him. Sam was still carrying his model sailing boat, of course, and Rosie had the kitten cuddled under her jumper. It had stopped squeaking now, because it was beginning to feel warm. Harry was playing in the garden.

'Hello,' he said in surprise. 'What have you come for? Are you going to let me have a look at your boat? Wow! It's fantastic!'

'No, we came to ask if you knew anything about tiny kittens,' said Sam. 'Someone threw one into the pond when we were there with my boat and I waded in and got it out. It's so wet and cold and miserable. We thought perhaps you'd know how we could feed it.'

'No, *I* don't,' said Harry. 'But the veterinary nurse who helps my father with the dogs here would tell you.'

'Will you ask her?' said Rosie.

A sly look came into Harry's eyes. 'Yes, if you lend me your boat to sail,' he said.

'I can't do that!' said Sam. 'I only had it today for my birthday!'

'Well, I won't ask the nurse for you then,' said Harry. 'Why don't you ask your mother? She'd know.'

'She doesn't want us to have animals yet, till our baby is older,' explained Rosie. 'Harry, don't be mean. The tiny thing is so frightened and miserable. We simply *must* get advice.'

'Tell Sam to lend me his boat and I'll go

straight away and ask the nurse,' said Harry.

Sam gave Harry the boat when he saw Rosie's eyes filling with tears. He could never bear to see his sister getting upset.

'All right. Here you are,' he said. 'But you are *mean*. I shall get into trouble with my father if he finds out that I've lent my boat to someone. Now go and ask the nurse.'

'You come with me,' said Harry, taking the big boat in delight. 'Honestly, isn't she wonderful! Has she got a name?'

'The *Flying Swan*,' said Sam in an angry voice. He thought Harry was being really horrible.

'Ugh! What a silly name! I shall call her *Snow-Maiden*,' said Harry.

'You won't! She's my boat,' said Sam, but Harry only laughed.

'Come on, bring the kitten,' he said. 'What a lot of fuss you make about a silly half-drowned creature. Look, there's Miss Morgan, the veterinary nurse. Go and ask her what you want to!' And he ran off, carrying Sam's lovely boat with him!

5

'Please tell us what to do!'

Miss Morgan, the veterinary nurse, was very busy. She had four dogs on leads, and was putting them into their kennels. She talked to them as she put them in.

'Now you be good, all of you. And Tinker, it's no use you barking the place down, you'll only upset the others. I'll take you all for another run this afternoon if you're quiet. And don't you try and bite that bandage off your leg, Lassie. Be a good dog now!'

The children waited until she had shut up all the dogs safely. They thought she sounded sensible and kind, and when she turned round they saw that she had a bright, smiling face.

'Hello,' she said. 'What do you want? Have

you come to see the vet? I'm afraid he's out at the moment.'

'No, we came to see Harry really,' said Sam, 'to ask him if he knew what we could do to help a half-drowned kitten. And he said we could come and ask you for some advice.'

'A half-drowned kitten! Whatever have you been doing to the poor thing?' said Miss Morgan, as Rosie drew it gently from the warmth of her jumper.

'Nothing!' said Sam. 'We didn't try to drown it! Someone came to the pond when we were sailing our boat and threw a bag into the water. And we saw the bag wriggling and I waded out to it...'

'And when we undid the bag, there was this tiny wet kitten inside, choking and spluttering,' said Rosie. 'It was so frightened and cold.'

'Poor little thing,' said Miss Morgan, and took it gently from Rosie's hands. 'It's in a bad way. It's been half starved by the look of it. And there's something wrong with one of its back legs.'

'PLEASE tell us what to do with it,' said Rosie, in tears. 'Will it live?'

'Oh yes, I think so,' said Miss Morgan. 'It's not shivering now, and by the sound of its little mew, it's very hungry. Come on, I'll show you how to feed it.'

She took them into the surgery, where the vet saw all his animal patients, and went to a cupboard. She handed Sam a tiny feeding bottle. 'There's some warm milk in that pan over there,' she said. 'I've been feeding a puppy with it, but there's enough left for this tiny mite. Pour some in the bottle, will you?'

Sam poured a little of the milk into the bottle and Miss Morgan took it from him.

'Open your mouth, kitty,' she said, and put the teat gently against the kitten's mouth. A drop of milk ran in and the kitten swallowed it. It mewed.

'Yes, it liked that,' said Miss Morgan. 'Come on, little kitty, take a few more drops. You'll soon feel better.'

The children watched Miss Morgan feeding the tiny creature, and were delighted to see how eagerly it swallowed the milk. Sam filled the little bottle twice more, and was allowed to feed the kitten himself. Then Rosie had a turn.

'Well, that's how you must feed it, until it can lap,' said Miss Morgan. 'Have you a bottle at home? I can give you one if you haven't.'

'Yes. Rosie's got her big doll's bottle,' said Sam. 'That'll do fine. But how will we know when the kitten is ready to lap, Miss Morgan?'

'It will lick a drop of milk off your finger,' said Miss Morgan. 'As soon as it does that, you can teach it to lap from a saucer. It will soon learn!'

'Its eyes aren't open,' said Rosie. 'Is it very, very young?'

'It's very, very small,' said Miss Morgan, 'small enough for its eyes still not to be open, but I think it's older than it looks. I expect it hasn't opened its eyes because it's weak and neglected. Are you sure you two can look after it?'

The children nodded. 'Yes!' said Sam. 'We can. Anyway, we're going to have a try. And who else would look after it if we didn't?'

'And what about its leg?' asked Rosie anxiously. 'The leg that hangs limp and doesn't move.'

'I think that'll soon mend,' said Miss Morgan. 'But if not, you can bring it back to me again. Now, keep the kitten somewhere warm. It will probably have felt shocked and chilled when it struggled in the cold pond water! I'm so glad you were there to save it.'

She gave the tiny kitten back to Rosie, who put it back under her warm jumper again.

'It's more like a white rat than a kitten!' said Miss Morgan. 'But it should grow up into a pretty little thing. You'd better take it home now.'

'Do we ... do we have to pay you anything for helping us?' asked Sam. 'I did lend Harry my model sailing boat, but you've done such a lot. We've got some birthday money you could have.'

'Bless you!' said Miss Morgan, smiling her nice smile. 'I'm glad to help, and there isn't anything to pay. It's your birthday, is it? Well, a very happy birthday to you! You've had a very unexpected birthday present, haven't you? A half-drowned kitten! Off you go then. Good-bye!'

The children set off down the path.

'She's nice, isn't she?' said Rosie. 'Let's buy her some chocolates sometime. I feel better about the kitten now, don't you? If it can take milk so easily it'll soon be all right. It feels so nice against me, under my jumper.'

'Rosie, do you think we'd better put it into the shed while it's so tiny?' asked Sam, as they walked off down the road. 'And don't you think we ought to give it milk in the middle of the night? You know Mummy gives the baby her bottle quite often, doesn't she? Morning, afternoon and night, and early in the morning too.'

'Well, we can't possibly creep out of the house in the middle of the night to feed the kitten,' said Rosie.

'No, we can't,' said Sam. 'Perhaps we'd better find somewhere near our bedrooms. What about the little boxroom? If the kitten made a noise no one would hear it there. And it's next to our bedrooms.'

'Yes, we could keep it in there till it doesn't need feeding at night,' said Rosie, cheering up. 'Honestly, I do wish we could tell Mummy about it! Don't you think we could?'

'No. It'd be mean of us to ask her to do something on our birthday-party day that she's already refused to do,' said Sam. 'She might think she'd got to have the kitten, and then it'd be a nuisance instead of something lovely. I think we should be able to manage it, Rosie. Let's try anyway.'

'But what about when it grows bigger?' said Rosie.

'Don't let's worry about that yet,' said Sam. 'We could give it away or ask the vet or something. The thing is, we've got to be kind to it now, and get it well and happy. Here we are, home at last! Now be careful nobody sees us, and asks you what that bump is under your jersey!'

They went quietly to the back door and peeped in. Nobody was there. They tiptoed in and went quietly upstairs.

'We'll go straight to the boxroom,' whispered Sam. And then they heard their mother's voice!

'Is that you, children? I wondered whatever had happened to you! Come and tell me what you've been doing this birthday morning!'

6

'What a good idea!'

The children looked at one another in horror and Rosie clutched the kitten more closely to her, hoping it would not make the tiniest sound.

'Run upstairs quickly,' said Sam, 'and find a place to put the kitten. I'll go and talk to Mummy.'

Rosie raced upstairs. She went into the tiny boxroom. The hot-water pipes ran through it to the radiator on the landing, so it was nice and warm.

'Just right for a cold little kitten,' thought Rosie. 'Now, what on earth can I give it for a bed?'

There was nowhere in the boxroom that would be soft and comfortable. Rosie wondered what to use for a cosy little bed. And then she suddenly thought of something. Yes! Her new doll's cot! It would be just the right size for a kitten.

She ran into her bedroom. The cot stood beside the toy box, and her baby doll was lying in it with her eyes closed. Rosie lifted her out and put her on a chair.

'This'll be just right,' she said, and went back into the boxroom with the cot. She put it down in a corner and took off the cot-clothes. She took out the sheets and left the little blanket, the pillow and the pink duvet. She put the tiny kitten onto the blanket and covered it up with the duvet.

'There,' she said. 'Now you lie there and go to sleep, kitten, and don't make any noise! You'll be quite safe here because nobody ever comes into this room.'

She heard footsteps running up the stairs. It was Sam.

'Rosie, where are you? Is everything all right?'

'Yes. Come and have a look,' said Rosie, and she took Sam into the boxroom. He laughed when he saw the tiny kitten in the cot.

'What a good idea! But that won't be big enough for it when it gets older. It could have my toy garage then, upside-down, with an old blanket inside. Or a cardboard box.'

'It's fast asleep,' said Rosie. 'It's quite dry now. Look, its fur is beginning to look nice and soft. How could anyone throw such a dear little thing away?'

'When do you think we ought to feed it again?' asked Sam. 'It's almost our lunchtime now. Shall we come up and feed it afterwards?'

'Yes. The baby always leaves a bit of warm milk in her bottle,' said Rosie. 'We can use that. Where's that little doll's feeding bottle of mine?'

'I saw it in your bedroom,' said Sam. 'I'll go and have a look. We'd better keep the box-room door shut, Rosie, in case anyone hears the little thing mewing. And we'd better bring up some old newspaper as well.'

They went down to have their lunch. It was nice to have a secret, but it would have been nicer still to share it with their mother and father!

'Well, birthday children,' said their father. 'Are you looking forward to your party? I've seen a magnificent cake out in the kitchen!'

'Yes. With eighteen candles on it!' said Rosie. 'It'll be amazing when I'm eighteen and Sam's twenty, Mummy! There'll have to be thirty-eight candles then!'

Afterwards their mother had to give Anne her bottle. 'Shall I give it to her for you, Mummy?' asked Rosie. 'I know you're busy. I've fed her before so I know how to do it.'

'All right. You can if you promise to be very careful,' said her mother. 'I'll get the baby for you and settle her on your knee and then I'll go and get her bottle ready.'

So very soon, there was Rosie sitting in her mother's low nursing chair, proudly giving the baby her bottle. Sam came to have a look.

'If she leaves any milk, let me have it for the kitten,' he said. 'It'll be nice and warm.'

'Well, get the milk jug from my dolls' tea-set,' said Rosie. 'I can pour it quickly in there when she's finished.'

Sam fetched the little jug. The baby seemed very hungry and was sucking at her bottle vigorously. Their mother popped her head in at the door to see that everything was all right.

'Honestly!' she said. 'She's almost finished her bottle already! Don't make her finish the last few drops if she doesn't want them. Can you put her back into her cot for me and play with her for a bit till I'm ready for her?'

'Yes, OK,' said Rosie. Her mother was right. The baby didn't want the last few drops, and Sam took off the baby's bottle teat and trickled the drops of milk into the little dolls' jug he had fetched.

'I'll go up to the kitten now,' he said. 'You come as soon as Mummy fetches the baby.'

He ran upstairs with the little jug and some newspaper. He went cautiously into the box-room. The kitten was still in the cot, but it was squirming about, wide awake, although its eyes were still fast shut. He picked it up carefully, sat down on the floor and put the tiny thing in the hollow of his crossed legs, on top of the newspaper. Then he tried to feed it just as the veterinary nurse had shown him. But the kitten was more lively now and didn't seem to know that there was milk about. Sam was very glad when Rosie came up to join him.

'You hold the kitten in your hands and I'll try and open its mouth enough to get the end of the teat in,' she said. And before long the kitten was eagerly drinking down the warm drops of milk that fell into its tiny mouth from the bottle.

'Wow! Isn't it hungry again?' said Sam. 'I don't think it'll be able to wait till the baby has her bottle at six o'clock.'

'Well, I've thought what we can do,' said Rosie. 'I'll go down to the kitchen and get a little bit of milk from the fridge. And we'll keep it up here, touching the hot-water pipes so that it'll always be warm. And then we can pop in here whenever we have a minute to see if the kitten would like a drink. Perhaps John and Sarah could come up too after the party and help.'

'What a great idea!' said Sam. 'Now look, the kitten's finished every drop of milk we brought up for it.'

'Mummy's calling us,' said Rosie. 'I expect she wants us to get ready for the party. It begins at half past three. I'll tuck the kitten up and then we'll go down. And if either of us has a chance to slip up here in the middle of the party to give the kitten a drink, we will.'

'You go and get some milk from the fridge then, while I go to help Mummy blow up the balloons,' said Sam. 'Leave it just there, by the hot-water pipes.'

He ran downstairs and Rosie followed. She heard him talking to their mother as she crept into the kitchen. She took a small cup from the cupboard and poured a little milk from it into the dolls' milk jug. She shut the fridge door carefully and went slowly back upstairs with the cup, careful not to spill even a drop.

'Here I am again, kitten,' she said, and put the cup against the hot-water pipes. 'Oh, you're asleep! You do look sweet with your head on the pillow. You look like a toy kitten, not a real one!'

Then down she went to get ready for the party. What an exciting day this was!

7

'It looks quite happy now'

The party began at half past three, when boys and girls began to come up the path to the front door. The boys looked clean and tidy in their jeans and shirts, and the girls were very pretty in their party outfits. Sam and Rosie gave them a great welcome.

'It's a pity we had to ask Harry to the party,' said Sam to Rosie, as they saw him coming up to the door.

'Yes, but we didn't know then that he was going to be so mean,' said Rosie.

'How's the kitten?' said Harry, as he came up to them.

'All right. And we haven't said anything about it yet, so don't *you* say anything either,' said Sam, afraid that Harry would give away their secret.

Then John and Sarah arrived, and the children were happy to leave Harry. Blast him! He had their boat, and their secret as well!

The party was lovely. All the children had brought little presents of sweets and chocolates, and admired the lovely things that the children had been given. Sam hoped that his mother wouldn't notice that his big model sailing boat wasn't amongst them! Whatever would he say if she asked him where it was? But she didn't. She was much too busy taking coats, and then starting off the games with musical statues and some disco music, to bother about anything else. And what fun the party was!

How exciting the tea was too. Their mother had made four different kinds of sandwich, three different kinds of cake besides the big birthday cake, and there was ice cream for everyone. There were five different kinds of crisps too! It was a great moment when the candles on the big cake were lit.

'Wow! Eighteen!' said John, grinning. 'Are you eighteen years old, Sam? You don't look it!'

'Don't be silly!' said Sarah. 'Sam's ten and Rosie's eight!'

Everyone laughed.

'He's older than you are now, anyway,' John said to Sarah. 'You're still only nine.'

After tea their mother asked if anyone would like to go upstairs to the bathroom.

'You take them upstairs if they do,' she said to Sam and Rosie. 'Then we'll play some more games.'

'Rosie, now's our chance to feed the kitten again,' said Sam in a low voice. 'I'll do it, shall I?'

Rosie nodded.

'Yes, but don't be too long. The bottle's next to the cup and the jug, standing near the hot-water pipes.'

Sam sped off to the little boxroom, taking John with him. They went in and shut the door. The kitten was squirming about in the dolls' cot, giving very small mews.

'Just coming,' said Sam to it, and went over to where Rosie had stood the cup of milk by the hot pipe. He poured some into the little bottle and went to the cot. The kitten smelt the

51

warm milk at once and mewed quite loudly. It swallowed drop after drop as Sam squeezed them out of the teat into its tiny mouth.

'Amazing!' whispered John. 'A kitten. How fantastic!'

'Shh,' said Sam. 'Mummy doesn't know yet.'

The kitten mewed again and Sam gave it some more milk.

'You're getting quite used to this performance, aren't you,' he said. 'There, that's enough, I should think. Now, we'd better get back to the party.'

He and John joined the others, and Sam gave Rosie a little nod that meant: 'Yes, the kitten's fed!' and she smiled back. The little creature had been at the back of her mind all the afternoon.

'Come upstairs with me later,' she whispered to Sarah. 'I've got something to show you.'

The party began again, with a video and afterwards a treasure hunt, which was very exciting. Every child was given the end of a long thread and told to follow it to the other end, where he or she would find a present. But very soon the threads began to get all tangled up and then the fun began!

'I think you've all found the wrong presents,' said Sam and Rosie's mother, laughing at the muddle. 'But never mind. You can change presents if you like.'

Nobody wanted to go home when the mothers and fathers arrived to fetch their boys and girls. Soon there was only Sarah and John left, as Aunty Eleanor was coming for them later. Harry hadn't gone yet either, and as no one ever fetched him he was very difficult to get rid of! Sam was afraid he would begin to talk about the boat and so he went off into the kitchen by himself.

'Now I've got to help Mummy with the baby,' said Rosie, firmly. 'Good-bye, Harry. I hope you enjoyed the party.'

'Well, you didn't have fruit salad,' said Harry. 'And I do like fruit salad.'

That was so like Harry. He went off at last and didn't even say, 'Thank you for a lovely time,' as all the others did.

Rosie flew up to the boxroom, calling out

to her mother that she wouldn't be a minute.
Sarah went with her and Rosie let her feed the
kitten. Sarah nearly burst with pride when
the kitten started to suck the milk from her.

'Isn't it lovely?' she whispered.

Rosie nodded.

'Yes, but please don't tell Aunty Eleanor yet,
will you?'

'No, not till you're ready,' said Sarah.

Then Sam and John came up as well and all
four children sat on the floor and took turns at
feeding the kitten.

'It looks quite happy now, doesn't it, Sam?'
said Rosie. 'Do you think it's forgotten the
shock it had this morning, when it was thrown
into the pond?'

'I expect so,' said Sam. 'It wasn't in the
water very long anyway. Mummy's calling you
now, Rosie. And haven't we had a great party!'

'Yes, wonderful,' said the other three, before
Rosie rushed off to help her mother.

'Would you like to feed the baby for me
again?' said her mother. 'I've rather a lot of
washing-up to do and she is always so good
with you. You do like feeding her, don't you?'

'Oh yes. Feeding babies and kittens is love-ly,' said Rosie before she could stop herself. Her mother was surprised.

'What do you know about feeding kittens?' she said, and went off to do the washing-up.

'I'll help you, Aunty Sue,' said Sarah quick-ly, who had come downstairs after Rosie, and wondered what else she might say!

'Honestly! I nearly gave our secret away,' thought Rosie. 'What a good thing Sam didn't hear me. He would've been cross! Although I bet Mummy would agree with me if she could only see our tiny kitten!'

'Well, did you enjoy your birthday?' asked their mother when the baby was safely back in her cot again, Sarah and John had gone home, and it was time for the children to go to bed. Rosie gave her mother a hug.

'It was wonderful!' she said. 'From the time we woke up this morning till this very minute now. Thank you for the super-fantastic party, Mummy. And wasn't the cake delicious?'

'It certainly was,' said Sam. 'Harry had four pieces!'

'Go and say good-night to Daddy,' said their

mother, 'and take some milk and biscuits up to bed with you for your supper. I'm sure you won't want anything more than that after your enormous tea.'

The children looked at one another when she said 'milk' and they both thought the same thing. They would save some of it for the kitten.

'What did you like best at the party?' asked Sam, as they went upstairs with their supper.

'Blowing all eighteen candles out at once!' said Rosie. 'I never thought we'd be able to do that! Now, let's just give the kitten its supper. And then it won't get any more until one of us wakes up in the night and goes to feed it. I hope we do. It'll be so hungry in the morning if we don't!'

8

'We haven't given it a name yet'

The children found the kitten fast asleep, and had to wake it up to give it its supper. It mewed as soon as it smelt the milk again. Sam stroked its soft fur.

'It was such an ugly little thing this morning,' he said. 'All wet and spiky fur. Now it's sweet, but look how thin it is. And I wish its back leg wasn't so useless. It doesn't seem to be able to use it at all when it tries to crawl.'

'Perhaps that's one reason why it was thrown away,' said Rosie. 'Perhaps its owner couldn't be bothered with a kitten whose back leg didn't work. Honestly, how would *he* like it if he broke an arm or a leg and was thrown into a pond to drown, instead of being taken to hospital!'

'You'd better get a move on, Rosie,' said Sam, 'or Mummy'll be coming up here before we've even got undressed! Now, if either of us wakes up in the middle of the night, we'll come and feed the kitten. Have you got your torch handy? You mustn't switch on any lights. We might wake Mummy and Daddy up if we do.'

'We'll each hide our torches under our pillows,' said Rosie. 'What an amazing kitten! Surely you can't drink any more milk! No. It's had enough now, so I'll tuck it up again. I think it knows us already, don't you, Sam?'

'Well, it knows the bottle of milk all right!' said Sam, with a grin. 'Give me the cup and I'll stand it by the hot water pipes again. That was a brilliant idea of yours, Rosie, it just warms the milk up nicely.'

The children were tired after their exciting day, and once they were in bed, they were soon fast asleep. Sam didn't wake up once during the night, but Rosie did. She sat up in bed in the dark. Now, what was it she had to remember if she woke up? Oh yes, of course! The kitten! She slipped out of bed with her torch, and was soon cuddling the mewing kitten and feeding it from the bottle of milk. It seemed strange to be sitting there in the dark box-room, with the light from the torch streaking across the floor where she had laid it down.

'I wish I could take you into bed with me and keep you warm,' she said to the kitten. 'There, I'll tuck you up in your cot again. I wonder if you miss your mother? I expect she's missing *you* and wondering where you've gone.'

Sam was quite upset next morning when he realized he hadn't woken up during the night. They were both quite amazed at the kitten in the morning because it seemed to have grown already.

'I think one of its eyes is trying to open,' said Rosie, looking at it closely. 'Yes it is! Look, Sam, can you see a crack between its eyelids? The right eye, see?'

'Yes, it *is* opening!' said Sam. 'Do you think it'll have pink eyes, because it's a *white* kitten, Rosie? When John and Sarah kept white mice, they all had pink eyes. Do you remember?'

'Yes. But I don't like pink eyes much,' said Rosie. 'I want it to have green eyes.'

'No, blue,' said Sam. 'A white kitten with blue eyes would be lovely. Come on. We'd better go downstairs. Mummy'll soon be wondering why we keep disappearing!'

It was a good thing it was the holidays because the children would never have been able to feed the kitten as often as they did, if they had had to go to school each day. As it was, they had to take it out of the boxroom after a few days, because their mother suddenly said that she was going to spring-clean the little room.

'Spring-clean it!' said Rosie, startled. 'But why, Mummy? It isn't untidy in there or anything, is it?'

'No. But I think there might be mice in there,' said her mother. 'There's a pile of old newspapers and I keep hearing little squeaks or something up on the landing, and the only place they could come from is the little boxroom. I expect some mice have made a nest in there out of the newspapers. I'm going to clean it out thoroughly tomorrow.'

The children had to make new plans for the kitten at once.

'The shed,' said Sam. 'That's the only place that's safe. No one goes in there now but us, as Daddy's got his new shed. I'll go out in the garden, Rosie, and if there's no one around, I'll whistle loudly. Then you can bring the kitten down at once. Can you wrap it up in a doll's shawl or something? Then it'll look as if it's a doll!'

Rosie ran up to the boxroom and wrapped the kitten in a little shawl. Then she heard Sam's whistle and ran downstairs. They got to the shed safely without being seen.

'Look, there's a cardboard box in here,' said Sam. 'Can you spare the shawl for a blanket? We could put some hay in the box under the shawl to make a nice soft bed. Did you bring the cup of milk? We shan't be able to warm it by the hot water pipes any more, but perhaps it won't matter now the kitten is getting bigger.'

Both the kitten's eyes were open now. They were a pale blue and the children hoped they wouldn't turn pink. It knew them quite well now, and had suddenly found out that it could purr! The children were surprised when they first heard it.

'Is it feeling ill?' asked Rosie, anxiously. 'Why is it making that funny noise?'

'Silly! It's purring for the first time!' said Sam. 'That means it's happy. What a funny little noise!'

It was beginning to crawl about too, although it still dragged one back leg behind it. Rosie felt the leg gently, but it didn't seem to be broken. Perhaps it would get right in time. It was a good thing too that Rosie had taken the kitten out of the boxroom straight away, because their mother changed her mind and began to clean it out that very morning.

'But I didn't find any mice,' she said. 'All the same, I did find something rather peculiar in the boxroom.'

'What was it?' asked the children.

'Your new doll's cot, Rosie,' said their mother. 'Whatever was it doing in there? Did your baby doll cry at night and wake you up, so that you put her in there?'

That made the children laugh. Then Sam changed the subject, afraid that Rosie wouldn't be able to explain about the doll's cot and would go red and make their mother curious.

They couldn't let the kitten be given away to anyone now, they really couldn't. And their mother might say that it would have to go, if she found out about it. But how could anyone help liking it? It really was so cute and pretty now.

The days went by and the kitten still lived in the shed and the children still fed it regularly. Once or twice they gave it bits of fish they had saved from their own dinner, and it gobbled them up. It had two rows of very small, pointed teeth and big blue eyes.

'They're going to turn green, I think,' said Sam. 'It'll be a lovely cat then, pure white with bright green eyes.'

'Do you realise we haven't given it a name yet?' said Rosie, rolling it over and over, and tickling its tummy. 'What shall we call it?'

'I don't know,' said Sam. 'It's got fine whiskers. Shall we call it Whiskers? Or Purry, because it's always purring?'

'No! Those aren't very good names,' said Rosie. 'Oh, look at it! It's rolled itself up into a white ball and it's chasing its tail. It looks like a snowball!'

'*That's* its name! Snowy!' said Sam, at once. 'Snowy, you'll have to learn your name! Snowy!'

'Miaow!' said Snowy, and ran to Sam.

'There,' he said. 'You know your name already, don't you, Snowy?'

9

'You're the meanest boy in the world'

That Saturday morning something very awkward happened. Sam's father announced that he would like to sail Sam's birthday model sailing boat with him.

'We'll take it down to the pond,' he said. 'There's a little breeze and the boat would sail well.'

But *Harry* still had the boat! He wouldn't give it back, even though Sam had asked him ever so many times.

'No,' he said each time. 'As long as I keep your secret about the kitten, you've got to lend me your boat. If you take it back, I'll tell about the kitten.'

'You're horrible and mean and unkind,' shouted Sam. He didn't like to see Rosie looking so worried either. But Harry only laughed.

And what on earth was he going to do now? Daddy wanted to go and sail the boat that very afternoon! Sam hunted about in his mind for some good excuse.

'But, Daddy, it's a long way to the pond, and it looks like rain,' he said, going very red.

'And Mummy asked me to take the baby in her pram to see Granny,' said Rosie, quite truthfully.

'Well, you can take the baby, and Sam can come with me,' said his father. 'A long way to the pond! I've never heard such nonsense! Don't you want to come, Sam?'

'Oh yes,' said poor Sam. 'I love going any-where with you, Daddy, you know that.'

'Well, we'll go then,' said his father. 'Go and get your boat and we'll have a look at her, and see if she's properly rigged.'

Sam looked at Rosie in despair. Harry had the boat, so he couldn't possibly go and get it. His father was puzzled.

'Well, Sam, please go along and get it,' he said, sounding impatient. 'I should have thought you'd have loved the chance of sailing that lovely boat. I don't think you've sailed it more than once, have you? I must say I've been rather surprised.'

Sam didn't know what to do. He turned as if to go and get his boat. Rosie looked frightened, because she was sure that her father was soon going to be very angry.

Sam turned round again, his face as red as fire. 'I can't go and get it, Daddy,' he said. 'It's not here.'

'Well, where is it then?' asked his father, astonished.

'Er, I lent it to Harry, you know, the vet's son,' stammered Sam. 'He ... he loves boats too.'

'You lent that beautiful boat to *Harry*, that careless boy?' cried his father. 'Whatever made you do a silly thing like that? Go and get it back at once!'

'Well, you see...' began Sam, and then didn't say any more, because that would have meant giving away the secret of the little white kitten. He stared miserably at his father.

'Well, either you go and get your boat back, or I go and get it,' said his father. 'And if I get it, I shall tell Harry what I think of him, for borrowing that beautiful boat. I told him he was *not* to borrow anything more from you, after he left those beautiful animal books of yours out in the rain all night.'

'I'll go and get the boat,' said Sam at once. Harry would certainly give away the secret if Daddy went round. He set off at once, hoping that Harry would not be mean. After all, he had had that lovely boat for ages now.

Harry *was* mean.

'You said I could have your boat as long as I kept your secret,' he said. 'And I'm still keeping your secret, so I'll still keep your boat. Of course, if you don't want me to keep your secret any longer, I won't.'

Sam stared at him, clenching his fists. He wanted to fight Harry at that moment. Harry saw the clenched fists and laughed.

'Of course you can have your boat just for today, but you'll have to pay me two pounds,' he said.

'You're the meanest boy in the whole world,' said Sam fiercely. He put his hand in his pocket and took out the Saturday pocket money that his father had given him that morning. He slammed it down on top of the wall.

'There you are! There's your money! Now give me my boat!'

Harry moved towards the money, but Sam clapped his hand over it.

'Oh no, you don't! You won't touch my two pounds until I have my boat,' he said.

Harry laughed and went into his house. He brought out the boat and handed it to Sam, snatching the money as he did so.

'You've tangled up all the rigging,' said Sam, angrily. 'And you've dented the keel.'

'That was done when you lent it to me,' said Harry at once.

'Liar!' said Sam, disgusted, and went off with his boat. How he detested Harry! Just because he and Rosie had wanted to help a half-drowned kitten, Harry had got him into all this trouble. Whatever would his father say when he saw the tangled rigging and the bent keel?

Sam's father had a great deal to say about the boat. He was very cross indeed.

'To think you've let this lovely boat get into this state in such a short time!' he said. 'Or did Harry do it? Yes, I suppose he did. Why in the world you lent it to him, I don't know! You know I don't like you to have too much to do with Harry. He's not a good friend for you. I'm very disappointed in you, Sam. I'm afraid it'll take so long to get the boat ready for sailing that it's not worth our while going.'

Sam couldn't bear to have his father so disappointed in him. 'I'm very sorry, Daddy,' he said.

'Well, look, go and buy some new string, and we'll rig the whole boat again,' said Daddy. 'I gave you two pounds this morning, didn't I?'

Sam put his hand in his pocket, and then remembered that he had given it to Harry, so that he could get the boat back. Oh no! Now he couldn't even go and buy the string.

'Now don't say you've spent all your money already,' said his father. 'You know you're supposed to save fifty pence a week in your money-box. Have you put that into it?'

'No, Daddy,' said Sam.

'Well, do you mean to say you've spent it all?' said his father. 'Not even ten pence left?'

'I've got ten pence left from last week,' said Sam desperately, and took it out. He simply didn't know what to say.

Rosie had been listening to all this, frightened and unhappy. She went to Sam, holding out her own two pounds.

'Sam can have my money,' she said. 'I've plenty in my money-box. You go and buy the string, Sam.'

'No,' said her father, giving the boat back to Sam. 'No. I don't feel as if I want to take Sam out with me today. I feel rather ashamed of him.' And he went indoors, without another word.

Poor Sam. He stared at Rosie, and then, afraid that he might cry, he rushed into the little shed, almost falling over Snowy the kitten.

'I don't believe it!' he said to the surprised kitten. 'Now what am I going to do?'

10

'You brave little thing!'

Sam's father wasn't at all pleased with him all that day and for several days afterwards. What made it worse was that John and Sarah had gone away for a few days with Aunty Eleanor and Uncle Jim. So Sam couldn't phone up John and ask him if he'd any string in his wood-work set to lend him.

Rosie said, 'Perhaps I could ask Sarah if she's got any string in her sewing set.'

'It's no good,' said Sam sadly, 'they aren't there. We'll just have to wait till they get back.'

Their mother heard about the spoiled boat too, and was sad that Sam had lent it to Harry.

'I should've thought you valued it too much to lend it to anyone before Daddy had even sailed it with you,' she said. 'You'll have to be specially good and helpful for the next week or two, so that Daddy won't feel so disappointed in you.'

Both the children were miserable, and, to make things worse, Harry was angry because Sam hadn't brought the boat back again.

'I can't,' said Sam. 'And I warn you, if I do, my father'll come round and get it back. And you'll get some tough things said to you. My father doesn't think much of you.'

So Harry didn't dare say much more. He was afraid of Sam's father. But he kept hinting that he was going to call in and see their mother.

'And I'll ask her how the kitten is getting on, shall I?'

Snowy was getting on brilliantly! He was a beautiful little creature now. His eyes were no longer blue, but as green as cucumbers, and very wide and bright. The only thing wrong with him was his back leg, which still dragged a little, though he could run quite fast on the other three. He could jump too, and the children laughed to see him pouncing after a cotton reel they tied to a bit of string.

Nobody knew he lived in the shed. When

their mother took the baby for a walk in her pram, the children let the kitten out and he played on the grass like a mad thing. He drank quite a lot of milk now and ate the bits of bread too that Rosie put to soak in the milk. Sometimes, for a treat, he had odd bits of fish or pudding that the children saved for him from their own plates.

'What are we going to do when he gets bigger?' said Sam. 'We can't keep him shut up all the time!'

'Honestly, I don't know,' said Rosie, taking the kitten into her arms. 'Look, Sam, there's a jackdaw down on the lawn again. I wonder if it's the one that flew off with Mummy's thimble the other day?'

'Yes, isn't it a nuisance!' said Sam, watching the big jackdaw strutting about on the grass. 'Did you see it take the thimble?'

'Yes,' said Rosie. 'Mummy had been sewing out here in the conservatory with the door open, watching the baby nearby in her pram. She went inside to answer the phone and left me with Anne. And suddenly the jackdaw flew into the conservatory, perched on the wooden table over there, and then flew off with Mummy's silver thimble!'

'And Mummy says that it must have seen her best brooch sparkling in the sun on her dressing-table,' said Sam, 'because that suddenly disappeared too. Daddy says jackdaws love taking bright things.'

The big black jackdaw strutted about, prying under bushes and pecking at a worm on the grass. And then, quite suddenly, Snowy leapt out of Rosie's arms and raced over the lawn, his bad leg dragging a little as he ran. The kitten was almost on the jackdaw before the big bird even saw him. With a loud 'chack-chack-chack!' the jackdaw rose in the air, and flew away at once. The children laughed at the kitten's surprise.

'You'll have to get used to birds flying off in the air,' said Sam. 'You brave little thing! The bird was much bigger than you!'

Snowy was very playful indeed. He grew more beautiful every day, and had a magnificent coat of soft, very white fur. He had learnt to wash himself now and spent a long time keeping himself as white as snow. He knew his

name and came running to the door of the
shed, mewing loudly, as soon as he heard the
children coming, calling to him in a low voice.
His mew became so loud that the children
began to be afraid their mother would hear
him when she came into the garden to put
Anne's pram out in the sun.

Sam felt worried.

'I'm afraid I'm still in trouble with Daddy,
and he'll be *really* angry if he finds out we've
been keeping a kitten a secret,' he said. 'Then
what'll happen to Snowy?'

'He'll be sent away somewhere,' said Rosie,
looking ready to cry. 'And he'll be so unhappy
because he loves us now.'

Well, of course, a kitten can't be kept secret
forever, and a day came when Snowy was dis-
covered! It happened very suddenly. Sam and
Rosie's mother was sitting out on the lawn
with the baby on a rug beside her, kicking
away happily.

The next-door neighbour, Mrs Janes, called
to her over the fence.

'How's that sweet little Anne of yours?'

Sam and Rosie's mother left her deckchair

and went over to the fence to have a chat. And then, on big black wings, the jackdaw came flying down on the grass. It saw baby Anne lying there, kicking, and it caught sight of something shining brightly in her hand. Her new silver rattle!

'Chack!' said the jackdaw, delighted to see the glittering thing, and it strutted up to the baby. It pecked at the silver rattle, but the baby wouldn't let go, staring at the black bird with big, frightened eyes. The jackdaw pecked again, and the baby yelled.

Their mother turned round at once and saw the pecking jackdaw. She gave a scream ... but before she could move towards the baby, someone else was there!

Snowy the kitten had seen the jackdaw from the window of his shed, halfway down the garden. His sharp eyes watched the bird as it went over to the baby, and then, scrambling and pushing, the kitten forced open the little window and leapt down, landing with a bump that really surprised him. He got back his breath and raced on three legs over to the rug where the baby lay, with the jackdaw pecking at the silver rattle. Snowy leapt at the big bird, and with a frightened 'chack-chack!' the jackdaw rose into the air, leaving one black feather in the kitten's mouth!

And then their mother was there, picking up Anne and comforting her.

'There, there,' she said. 'Naughty bird to come and frighten baby! And where on earth did that brave little kitten come from? It just scared the jackdaw away before it pecked *you*, Anne!'

She sat down on the rug and the kitten crept onto her skirt and lay there. Their mother stroked it.

'You dear pretty little thing. I wonder who you belong to?'

At that moment the children ran down the garden to tell their mother about the shopping they'd just been doing. And how surprised they were to see her stroking the little white kitten! They stood still in amazement.

'Look, darlings,' said their mother. 'Look at this little pet of a kitten! That jackdaw came down and saw the baby's shining silver rattle, and began to peck at it, and frightened Anne so much. And this tiny thing appeared from somewhere and drove the bird away. I do wonder who it belongs to. Isn't it sweet?'

'Yes, he is sweet,' said Rosie, not knowing what to say. 'He's a darling.'

'We must find out who the owner is,' said their mother. 'You can fetch the kitten a saucer of milk. It really did save the baby from being badly pecked and frightened. I *do* wish it was our kitten! I wouldn't mind having one like this, I really wouldn't!'

The children could hardly believe it!

'Mummy, do you really mean that?' asked Sam at once. 'Do you *really* wish it was ours?'

'Yes,' said his mother. 'It's a most lovable little thing. Look at it cuddling up to me. Do you know whose it is?'

'Yes!' said Rosie. 'Yes, we do know. It's *ours*, Mummy. Sam's and mine! Oh, please, can we keep it? Oh, please, do say we can!'

11

'And now he's really ours!'

When their mother heard Rosie say that the kitten belonged to her and Sam, she couldn't believe it at all. She stared at the children in astonishment.

'Now what exactly do you mean by that?' she said. 'The kitten can't be yours! I've never seen it before. Tell me all about it at once, please!'

So, taking the kitten on her knee, Rosie told her mother how they had rescued the little thing from drowning, and how they had gone to ask Harry if he could help them with the kitten because his father was a vet.

'And that's when I had to lend Harry my boat,' said Sam, 'because he wouldn't help us with the kitten unless I did! Miss Morgan, the veterinary nurse, told us how to look after him.'

'We couldn't tell you because we knew you didn't want a puppy or a kitten till Anne could walk,' said Rosie. 'But, Mummy, he was such a poor, poor little kitten, so wet and cold and thin and hungry, we simply had to take him home.'

'Darling Rosie,' said her mother, and put her arm round the little girl, 'I'm so glad you did what you did. I'd have done it too. Poor little kitten! How could anyone be so cruel? And to think that, small as he is, he chased that big jackdaw away. Just think, that bird could have pecked the baby very badly.'

'Mummy, do you really like the kitten then?' asked Sam, eagerly. '*Will* you let us keep him? He's growing bigger now and it was getting difficult to hide him. You did say you wished he was ours, didn't you?'

'Yes, I did. And I meant it,' said his mother, stroking Snowy gently. 'What a beautiful little creature he is. But we must do something about his leg. Perhaps your father will take him to the vet.'

'Do you think Daddy'll still feel disappointed in me, when he finds out it was because of the kitten that I had to lend Harry my new boat?' asked Sam, anxiously.

'He'll be proud of you, Sam, I can promise you that,' said his mother. 'You're two good, kind children, and any mother would be proud of you. We'll tell your father as soon as he gets home. Oh, just look at the kitten! He's cuddling up in my skirt again. He really does belong to us, doesn't he!'

The children were very, very happy. Secrets were fun, but this one had become very worrying, especially after their father had found out about the boat being lent to Harry. It was lovely to feel that the kitten could be with them now whenever they wanted.

'We'll be ever so careful not to let Snowy get under your feet, Mummy,' said Rosie. 'I'll put him into my room whenever you've got to carry the baby upstairs.'

'Oh, he seems such a sensible little thing, I'm sure he won't trip me up,' said her mother, who really did think Snowy was wonderful. 'I'm longing to tell Daddy all about it.'

Their father was *most* astonished when he heard the story. He sat and listened as the children and their mother told him all about it, shaking his head in amazement.

'A kitten! And he's been here such a long time and we never guessed!' he said. 'No wonder Mummy thought there were mice squeaking in the boxroom. Let me hold him for a minute. He looks a pet!'

The kitten sniffed at their father's hands and then settled down on his knee, purring loudly.

'There! He knows he belongs to you too,' said Rosie, delighted. 'Just listen to him purring. That's his way of telling you, Daddy!'

'I understand about the boat now, Sam,' said his father, stroking Snowy. 'And although I told you off about it, I think it was kind of you to give up something you were proud of in order to get help for the kitten. I'll have a few words to say to Harry about that, though!'

'There's something wrong with his leg,' said their mother. 'He drags that back one a bit. We must have it seen to before it stiffens up permanently.'

'We'll take him straight round to the vet this

morning,' said their father. 'I'll telephone them to say we're coming. Hold the kitten, Sam, will you?'

'Daddy, you're not still disappointed in me, are you?' asked Sam, anxious that everything should be absolutely right between him and his father again. It had bothered him very much when he felt his father wasn't proud of him.

'Disappointed! I'm only sorry I didn't understand what was happening,' said his father, putting his arm round Sam's shoulders. 'I wouldn't have shouted at you at all if I'd known, you know that. I'm prouder of you and Rosie too, than I ever was before!'

Sam and Rosie's father took the kitten round to the vet, and Sam and Rosie went with him. The vet was kind and gentle, and examined the stiff little leg carefully.

'Leave him with me overnight,' he said. 'I'll have to manipulate the leg a little. I can put it right, but I may have to send the kitten to sleep while I do it. When he wakes up, his leg'll hurt a little, but it'll be quite all right in a few days.'

'Oh, thank you,' said Rosie, delighted. 'Isn't he a lovely kitten, Mr Williams?'

'He's lovely,' said the vet, stroking Snowy. 'I can't think how anyone could have been foolish enough, as well as unkind enough, to throw him into a pond. This is a kitten that could win a prize any day, when he grows up. I suppose they didn't want a kitten with a bad leg! Well, leave him with me for now.'

'Thank you,' said the children's father. 'Now, could I have a word with Harry, please. Where is he?'

'In the garden somewhere,' said the vet. 'Oh, and will you tell my next client to come in please, as you go out? And don't worry about the kitten. He'll be fine by tomorrow!'

They all went out.

'Call Harry,' said Sam's father to him. 'Look! There he is.'

Sam called out loudly.

'Harry! Harry, you're wanted!'

Harry came running up eagerly, hoping that he could perhaps get some more money out of Sam. He stopped very suddenly when he saw the children's father.

'Come here, please, Harry,' said Sam's father. 'I've got something to say to you. No, don't run away, unless you'd rather I said it to your father.'

That made Harry come back at once, his face as red as a beetroot. He stood sulkily on the garden path.

'Take that scowl off your face,' said the children's father. 'You know very well what I'm going to say to you, don't you? I know all about your mean behaviour over the boat, and how you made Sam give you his money. I'll not tell your father this time. But NEXT time, there'll be serious trouble. Do you understand?'

'I'll, I'll give you back the two pounds,' mumbled Harry, very scared indeed. 'Don't tell my father. He'll ground me and I hate being in my bedroom all by myself. Shall I go and get the money now?'

'You can give it to Sam tomorrow,' said the children's father. 'He'll be coming round to fetch the kitten. And remember, any more of this kind of thing, and you'll find yourself in real trouble!'

They went out of the gate and left Harry shaking in his shoes. How awful! To think that

Sam and Rosie's father knew all about his meanness! Harry made up his mind at once that he'd never do anything like it again. What on earth would happen if his own father got to hear about it?

It was a happy little family that went home that afternoon. The children hung on their father's arm and told him every single thing about the kitten.

'And now he's really ours!' said Rosie, happily. 'Oh I do hope his leg'll soon be better. Won't Anne love him when she's a bit bigger, Daddy?'

'Oh, we'll all love him,' said her father. 'It looks as if Snowy's going to be the happiest kitten in the world. But how you managed to keep your secret so well, I really don't know!'

'Daddy,' said Sam, 'please can we phone John and Sarah and tell them all about Snowy and his leg? They helped us to feed him after our party and they really wished they had a kitten too.'

'Yes,' said Rosie, 'and we can tell them about Harry and the boat, and what the vet said about the kitten's leg getting better soon.'

'And don't forget to tell them about how Snowy saved baby Anne from being pecked,' said their mother. 'He really is the best kitten in the world.'

12

'One good turn deserves another! Purr-purr-purr!'

Next morning the children went to fetch the kitten from the vet's. Harry was at the gate, waiting for them.

'Here's the money,' he said, pushing it into Sam's hand. 'I'm sorry for what I did.' And then away he went before they could say a word.

Sam looked at Rosie.

'He sounded as if he really meant it,' he said.

'Yes,' said Rosie slowly. 'Perhaps one day we can ask him round to play with Snowy.'

'Hello, children,' called Miss Morgan, the veterinary nurse. 'The vet's gone out to see a horse that's had an accident. Anyway, here's your kitten. It's amazing how he's grown since you first brought him here. He's beautiful, isn't he?'

'What about his leg?' asked Rosie, anxiously, stroking Snowy as he lay in the veterinary nurse's arms.

'Quite all right,' said Miss Morgan. 'It'll feel a bit bruised for a day or two, so don't be surprised if he still limps a little. But he'll soon be running around on all four legs, and if I know anything about it, he'll be a real little monkey!'

'Dear little Snowy,' said Rosie, and the kitten looked at her out of his big green eyes, and purred loudly as she took him from Miss Morgan. 'You're going to belong to the whole family now, instead of just to Sam and me.'

'You know, this kitten must have come from quite a good litter of kittens,' said Miss Morgan. 'He's really beautiful. If I were you, I'd enter him for the Kitten Section of the Cat Show when it's held in a few weeks. He might win a prize for you.'

'Really?' said Sam, in delight. 'Do you hear that, Snowy? You might win a prize. How would you like that?'

The kitten mewed and Miss Morgan laughed.

'He says he'd like it very much, if he gets something to eat out of it!' she said. 'Well good-bye for now. I've got about twelve pups to see to, and a few cats, a guinea pig and some rabbits. I must go and see to my big family at once.'

On the way home the children called at their cousins' cottage and showed off Snowy to them. John picked him up carefully and stroked him.

'You do look happy now,' he said. 'I can't imagine what you must have looked like when Sam and Rosie pulled you out of the old flour bag.'

'Oh, don't remind him,' said Rosie anxiously. 'He'll never ever want to remember that day again.'

'Oh, I expect he's forgotten all about it now,' said Sarah sensibly. 'After all, he must be the best-looked-after kitten in our road!'

And all the four children burst out laughing.

In two days' time the kitten's leg was perfectly strong, and he could run on all fours instead of only on three legs. Now that Sam and Rosie's mother knew about him he had the run of the house, and was soon at home everywhere. Anne loved him and he was as gentle as could be with her, never putting out a single claw. Sam and Rosie's mother didn't fall over him once, even though he liked to hide under the beds and chairs, and leap out at any passing feet.

'It's really quite easy to watch out for him,' she said. 'I was silly not to let you have one before. Perhaps we could have a puppy next, while Snowy is still a kitten. Then they could grow up together.'

'For Christmas!' said both the children at once.

'A black one, and we'll call it Sooty,' added Sam. 'Snowy and Sooty! That'd be fun!'

One day Sam's father took him down to the pond to sail his boat, and how beautifully it sailed there, tugging at its string. All its rigging had been renewed, and the keel had been mended. Sam was very proud when he saw so many boys coming up to watch the *Flying Swan*. On the way home Sam spotted a big notice in a shop.

'Look, Daddy,' he said. 'The Cat Show is on

next month, and there's a class for kittens. Miss Morgan said Snowy was a fine kitten and that we ought to put him in for the Cat Show. Can we? Oh, do say we can! I know John and Sarah would like to come too and they could help us get him ready.'

'Well, of course,' said his father. 'I'll be very surprised if there's a prettier kitten than our Snowy! WHAT a good thing you were sailing your boat on the pond when the poor little thing was thrown into the water!'

'Yes! And how surprised that person would be if he, or she, could see the kitten now,' said Sam. 'Come on, let's get home as quickly as we can and tell Rosie all about the Cat Show.'

Rosie was very excited. She picked up Snowy and patted him.

'We'll brush you and give you a lovely green ribbon to match your eyes,' she said. 'Do try and win a prize, Snowy, even if it's only a little one. We'd be prouder still of you then!'

John and Sarah came round the same afternoon. They all decided to walk down the hill to the pet shop and buy the ribbon, a collar, a bell and a name-tag. 'I've got my two pounds pocket money,' said Rosie.

'And I've got four pounds,' said Sarah. 'I'd like to give it to Snowy. He deserves it.'

'I can give you two pounds too,' said Sam.

Only John looked worried.

'I've spent all my money on sweets,' he said, going red.

'It serves you right,' said Sarah crossly.

'I know,' said Rosie, 'why doesn't John share his sweets with us all while we walk down the hill? That'd be sort of helping Snowy!'

Everyone cheered up and John said,

'Yes. I'll go and get them at once. Lovely toffees we can suck!'

By the time the Cat Show came, Snowy was the funniest, most mischievous kitten that any of them had ever seen. Sam and Rosie's father said he had never laughed so much in his life as he had since Snowy arrived in the family.

'He saw himself in the mirror yesterday,' said their father, 'and thought it was another cat there. So he tried to make friends with it, and purred loudly and patted the glass. Then when the kitten in the mirror wouldn't make friends, he flew at it and tried to bite it. And then he couldn't think why he got his nose bumped so hard!'

On the day of the Show Rosie brushed Snowy till his coat gleamed like the snow itself. Then she tied the green ribbon round his neck to match his eyes.

'You look good enough to have your picture on a calendar,' she said. 'Mummy, isn't he lovely? Do you think he'll win a prize? We've entered him in the "White Kitten" class and the "Prettiest Kitten" class as well.'

'He won't get a prize in the "White Kitten" class,' said her mother, 'because usually kittens belonging to Prize Pedigree Cats win those prizes. But he might win a "Prettiest Kitten" prize. You've certainly made him look gorgeous, Rosie!'

Very proudly the children carried Snowy to the Cat Show in a closed basket with a handle. They met John and Sarah there with their mother and father.

'Hello!' called Rosie. 'Isn't this exciting! Come on, you two! Let's go and find the place where we have to leave Snowy.'

They all entered his name in the 'White Kitten' class and the 'Prettiest Kitten' class too. He was put in a cage alongside many other cages of kittens. And how strange, next to him was a kitten almost EXACTLY like him! The man in charge of it stared at Snowy in surprise.

'Where did you get that kitten?' he said. 'It might be the twin of mine!'

Sam told him.

'Somebody threw him into the pond to drown him and we rescued him. He had a bad leg, poor little thing, and we think that was why he was thrown away.'

'A bad leg!' said the man, and turned and said something to the boy with him. Sam, John, Rosie and Sarah couldn't help hearing what he said.

'Do you suppose that's the one we didn't want, because of the leg, Leonard? It's the living image of ours here, green eyes and all.'

'Sh!' said the boy, and frowned at the man. 'They'll hear you.'

The children had all heard him of course, and they looked at one another in disgust. Was *this* the boy who had tried to drown their kitten?

Soon the judges came along, and they exclaimed in delight when they saw Snowy. And then they saw the white kitten in the next cage, so exactly like him. They examined them both carefully, and scribbled notes on their cards. Then they passed on.

And when the prize winners' names were called out over the microphone, Snowy had won *both* the Kitten Prizes: first prize in the 'White Kitten' class and the first prize in the 'Prettiest Kitten' one as well. The children could hardly believe it.

'Three cheers!' called Sarah at the top of her voice and the other three joined in.

'Did you hear that, Snowy?' said Rosie, putting her hand into the kitten's cage and stroking his soft fur. 'You've won two prizes! You've beaten all the other kittens!'

The man and the boy who owned the kitten in the next cage were angry, for they thought their own kitten would easily win. They glared at Snowy.

'Just because its eyes are greener than our kitten's,' said the boy. 'I wish I'd drowned it properly.'

'Well, it serves you right!' said Rosie unexpectedly, remembering again the tiny, wet, frightened little thing that Sam had rescued from the pond. 'It just serves you RIGHT!'

'I don't know what you are talking about, you silly little girl,' said the man. But he did, of course!

'You leave her alone,' said John, coming up. 'Or I'll tell my Dad!'

With a sneer the man and the boy walked away, taking their kitten in its cage with them.

'Well, they won't dare come back,' said Sam, 'because if they do they know our parents will report them to the RSPCA!'

The children carried Snowy home in triumph, and the prizes too. Twenty whole pounds: ten for each win, and cards to say that Snowy was the 'Prettiest Kitten in show' and the 'Best White Kitten in show' as well.

'We'll buy you a lovely basket of your own with a cushion inside,' said Rosie joyfully.

Sam and Rosie's mother was delighted with Snowy. She cuddled him and he patted her with his tiny paw.

'You'll certainly have a new basket of your

very own,' she said, and the kitten mewed loudly and purred.

'What did you say?' she said. 'You want Rosie to buy herself a pretty ring, and Sam a new railway signal for his electric train? Well, that's kind of you, Snowy! I'll give them back ten pounds of the prize money. Here you are, children.'

Snowy mewed again.

'Oh, and you think there should be some sweets as well for the Fabulous Four to share? What a good idea!'

'But, do you really think Snowy wants us to have all that?' asked Rosie, pleased.

'Of course! He loves you, doesn't he?' said her mother. 'And I'm sure I know what he's purring to you this very minute. Listen! Can't you hear him purring, "One good turn deserves another, purr – purr – purr!"'

Snowy jumped onto Rosie's shoulder and purred in her ear, rubbing his head against her, and then he jumped onto Sam's and did exactly the same.

'He's telling us again,' said Rosie. 'All right, Snowy. We'll share your prize money. Thank you very, very much. Oh Mummy, don't you wish someone could tell the story of our Birthday Kitten? I do!'

Well, I've told it. And now there's nothing more to say except a few words from Snowy himself.

'Purr – Purr – Purr – Purr!'

Four in a Family

John and Sarah's Dad is in hospital after a serious accident and they'd love to take him some presents. The only problem is they don't have any money!

Together with their cousins, Sam and Rosie, they begin to make plans. The Fabulous Four are full of ideas about how they can earn some money, but will they really manage it? And what is Rosie's secret for earning the most?

Read on to see what becomes of their ingenious plans.

Available from October 2000:

The Hidey Hole

It's blackberry picking time, and Sam, Rosie and John go out to the common. But when they get there, they see that all of the bushes have already been picked. Then they discover a better place to go blackberrying – the neighbour's garden! And to their surprise, they find an amazing hidey hole there.

What do they find inside it? And who has been using it as a secret place?

The Very Big Secret

Sam and Rosie's Mum has had to go away for a few days and has promised to bring them back a wonderful present.

In the meantime, the two of them decide to go down to the meadows and search for honeysuckle by the stream. But when they come back, Rosie finds something incredible. What has she found? And how on earth did it get there?

Read on to see how Rosie and Sam solve their dilemma, and what Mum's wonderful present will be.

The Four Cousins

The Fabulous Four learn about some children who can't afford a holiday and decide to help. They all start doing jobs to earn money, but Sarah and John soon turn to reading or snoozing instead of working hard. But when they hear how much money Sam and Rosie have saved up, they try to earn their own share.

Will the four cousins be able to earn enough for the holiday? What will be their wonderful reward?